SPUDDY II

The Potatoes are Back

SPUDDY II

The Potatoes are Back

Pat Hill

Illustrations by
Jan Bryant

The Book Guild Ltd
Sussex, England

The Book Guild Ltd
25 High Street
Lewes, Sussex

First published 1997
© Pat Hill 1997
Set in Souvenir Light
Typesetting by Acorn Bookwork, Salisbury

Origination, printing and binding in Singapore
under the supervision of
MRM Graphics Ltd, Winslow, Bucks

A catalogue record for this book is available from the British Library

ISBN 1 85776 277 0

CONTENTS

BOOK 1
SPUDDY HELPS
FATHER TRICKMAS

1

THE MAN IN THE MOON

The ground was very hard when Dog woke. He opened one eye and twitched his nose. He could see Speedy the horse's breath streaming out of his nostrils as he cropped the frosty white grass.

Dog opened one eye and twitched his nose.

'Good morning, Speedy,' said Dog, yawning.

'SShh. Can you hear something?'

'Yes. It's someone calling,' said Dog.

Speedy started to walk towards the ploughed field where the noise seemed to be coming from. The ground was so hard and icy that his hooves slipped and slithered all over the place, his legs splaying out in all

His legs splayed out in all directions.

directions. Dog's paws weren't so slippy, having hairs in between his toes, but he too found it difficult to keep upright. They reached the field and stopped. 'Listen,' said Speedy.

It was very cold and very quiet. Except for the crackle of the trees as the frost bit the branches, there wasn't a sound. Yes there was! A faint but distinct calling came from under the ground. 'Get me out, dig me up. I must be free,' said the voice.

Dog went over to where the potato shoots were showing. One was trembling. Dog put his ear to the ground. 'It's Spuddy,' he said, and he began to dig. It was so hard that even Dog found it difficult to scrape away the frost from the earth.

'Here, let me help,' said Speedy the horse. 'I'll breathe warm air through my nostrils and melt the frost while you dig.'

Speedy and Dog worked hard, Speedy snorting warm breath, and Dog digging. At last a hole was beginning to appear.

Suddenly, Spuddy put his head above the ground. 'Hello,' he said. 'Thanks, Dog. Now quick, we haven't much time.'

'Much time, much time. Much time for

'I'll breathe warm air through my nostrils and melt the frost.'

what?' said Speedy.

'You'll see,' replied Spuddy, shivering in the cold. 'Dog, I need my red jacket from your kennel, and a warm muffler for my neck. It's very cold above ground, isn't it?'

'What about the others?' said Dog.

'Oh, leave them, they'll sleep the winter through,' Spuddy went on, 'but we have something very important to do.'

'What?' said Speedy the horse.

6

'Wait and see,' and Spuddy stuck out his tummy and smiled mysteriously.

First they fetched Spuddy's red jacket with the spotted handkerchief in the top pocket from Dog's kennel, and found a warm muffler for his neck. Spuddy jumped on to Speedy's back.

'Dog, jump up beside me, and hold on.'

7

'Now Speedy, you see that light in the sky. Just follow it. Dog, jump up beside me, and hold on.' Speedy gave a leap towards the light and found himself on a cloud flying through the air. 'I'm flying,' Speedy cried. 'It's magic,' shouted Spuddy.

'Hooray,' laughed Dog as he held his breath, his ears flapping up and down as they sped higher and higher into the sky.

Thump. Crash, they landed with a thud on the light and Spuddy and Dog rolled off Speedy's back.

'Hello,' said a deep voice, 'I am the Man in the Moon, and you have just landed on me. In a minute Father Trickmas will join us.'

'Who is Father Trickmas?' said Speedy the horse, climbing off the cloud.

'Oh, just a friend,' said the Man in the Moon, smiling.

'I am the Man on the Moon, and you have just landed on me.'

9

2

FATHER TRICKMAS

Swoosh. Thud. A huge sleigh pulled by 28 reindeer carrying a very large man whizzed through the air and landed on the moon. The man wore a red coat trimmed with fur and he had whiskers all over his face which were white with frost. His eyes shone so bright they sparkled in the moonlight, which made him see far and wide.

'Hello,' he said, smiling all over his frosty face. 'I'm Father Trickmas, and I'm delighted to see you, Spuddy. You are a very special potato.'

Spuddy stuck out his tummy. He liked being called a very special potato.

'Did you hear me calling to you when you were buried under the ground?'

'Oh, it was you,' said Spuddy. 'I knew I was wanted but I wasn't sure why.'

'I am even more pleased to see you have

'I am Father Trickmas, and I am delighted to see you!'

11

put on your red jacket with the spotted handkerchief in the top pocket, and you have a red muffler round your neck. You look a bit like me, which is very important,' said Father Trickmas. 'Did you know that your face has turned frosty-white, and your eyes are bright and sparkling to make you see far and wide like mine?' laughed Father Trickmas.

'He is quite right,' said Dog.

'Well, your hair is frosty-white, and so are the tips of your ears,' replied Spuddy. 'It looks rather nice.'

'Am I frosty-white too?' said Speedy the horse.

'Yes, you're frosty-white too,' said Dog kindly.

'What is the matter with your head?' said Speedy the horse, looking at one of the reindeer. 'Your branches are drooping.'

'I have got a headache,' replied the reindeer gloomily. 'My antlers have broken, they are not branches, and I am feeling very ill.'

'They look like branches to me' said Speedy.

'Don't be rude,' said Dog. 'They are not branches they are antlers.'

12

'I have got a headache,' replied the reindeer gloomily.

'Poor thing,' said Spuddy. 'I know what it's like to have a headache. I get one from time to time, and when I do I have to go under the ground. It's the only cure.'

'I can't go underground,' said the reindeer.

'No you can't,' said Speedy the horse.

'What you need are some new branches.'

'Antlers,' muttered Dog under his breath.

'I am in a spot of bother,' interrupted Father Trickmas. 'As you can see, one of my reindeer is sick and I'm all behind.'

'Behind what?' said Spuddy, glancing about him.

'Taking the presents round.'

'Round where?' said Spuddy, looking again.

'The world, my friend, the world,' replied Father Trickmas. 'See my sack? It is full of toys for all the children of the world, and I only have two more days to deliver them. That is why I need you, all three of you. Speedy,' he went on, 'would you take the place of my sick reindeer and help to pull my sleigh?'

'I'd love to,' said Speedy the horse. 'Do I have to have branches on my head?'

'No,' laughed Father Trickmas. 'You will do as you are. Now Spuddy,' he went on, 'if I give you half my toys, would you go your way far and wide, and I will go my way far and wide. We will visit far-off places and then I will meet you back here in a couple of days.'

'How will we know how to get back here?' said Spuddy, looking rather anxious.

'Your magic cloud will guide you, and if you take my sick reindeer with the drooping antlers, he will fill your sack with toys and you can deliver them. Even if his head does ache he still knows the way round the world.'

'Easy,' nodded the reindeer with the drooping antlers, being careful they did not drop off, as they were rather loose and very sore.

Dog had kept quiet until now, sitting on the moon beside Spuddy.

'Dog, could you lift and carry this sack in your mouth and take it round the world with Spuddy?' said Father Trickmas.

'Certainly,' said Dog, pleased to be involved in this strange adventure.

Father Trickmas stuffed toys into a sack and carefully handed it to Dog. Dog leant over, nearly falling off the moon as he did so, and grabbed the sack in his teeth.

'That was close,' said Spuddy. 'If you had fallen off the moon you'd have had a long way to go back to earth on your own. I'm sure you'd have landed with a terrible bump

15

and hurt yourself.'

'I know,' said Dog. 'I will have to be careful,' and he dropped the sack on to the cloud and leapt after it, ready to take off.

'Jump on the cloud, sick reindeer with the drooping antlers,' cried Father Trickmas. 'You too, Spuddy, and off you go. I will see you in two days. Goodbye.' With that, Spuddy, Dog and the reindeer with the drooping antlers swept off the moon on their cloud. They waved goodbye to Father Trickmas and his 27 reindeer, and Speedy the horse, who was pawing the moon, impatient to be away, and tossing his head in the air. His nostrils were steaming as he puffed and snorted.

'Don't be so impatient,' laughed the Man in the Moon.

'I can't help myself. I love speed, you see. That's why I'm called Speedy the horse.'

3

DOWN THE CHIMNEYS

'Now,' said Spuddy, 'let's arrange ourselves properly on this cloud. Come on, reindeer, you sit in front and guide us on our way, and we will sort out these toys and get them delivered.'

The reindeer with the drooping antlers spoke to the cloud and it started to float gently down towards the earth. There were a lot of lights below them.

'This must be a town,' said Spuddy. 'Get ready to jump, Dog. Wait for us here, reindeer – we will be back in a bit.' Dog carried the sack in his mouth as they drifted down and landed on the roof of a house.

'Quick, Dog, down the chimney,' said Spuddy.

'Down the chimney!' Dog exclaimed in amazement.

'Yes, that's what Father Trickmas does,'

They landed in a room which had lights twinkling on a Christmas tree.

said Spuddy, sticking out his tummy.

'Oh well, there is always a first time,' said Dog as he slid down the chimney with the sack in his mouth, followed by Spuddy. They landed in a room which had lights twinkling on a Christmas tree.

'That looks pretty,' said Spuddy.

'Yes *it* does but *you* don't,' laughed Dog.

'What do you mean?'

'You aren't white any more, Spuddy, and your jacket. Oh dear.'

Spuddy looked down and all he saw was a black sooty jacket. The spots had gone from his handkerchief in his top pocket and he was black all over.

Dog began to sneeze. He shook his ears and black dust escaped from his woolly coat. Soon everywhere was sooty. As they climbed the stairs and crept into the bedroom they left black footprints behind them.

'Never mind,' said Spuddy, 'the children will know where we have come from, and why we have come.'

At the bottom of each bed hung a woolly sock. 'Dog, you fill that sock and I will fill this one.'

Dog peered at the sleeping child and felt

Dog peered at the sleeping child.

in the sack with his nose. He pulled out a large coloured ball and squeezed it into the sock. It stuck out at the top and Dog tried to nudge it further down.

'Come on, Dog, hurry,' whispered Spuddy. 'We've got a lot to do.'

Dog picked up the sack and they crept down the stairs and up the chimney once more. The only sign that they had been, were the sooty footprints they had left behind on the staircase and passage leading to the children's bedroom.

The reindeer with the drooping antlers was sitting on the cloud waiting for them.

All night long Spuddy and Dog went from house to house. Sometimes they climbed down chimneys, and sometimes they didn't. They just seemed to go through the windows and doors without even opening them. If it was dark, Spuddy's eyes shone extra bright to light them on their way, and he stuck out his tummy with pride. They worked all through the night, the next day and the next night.

Every time they returned to the cloud the reindeer with the drooping antlers filled the sack with more toys, and they went on their way.

Once when they returned to the cloud and Dog gave the sack to the reindeer, he asked, 'Why do we never run out of toys?'

'Magic,' replied the reindeer with the drooping antlers.

'Why can we go through doors and windows without opening them?' said Spuddy.

'Magic,' said the reindeer, once more

filling the sack and handing it to Dog, who picked it up in his mouth.

One town they came to had so many lights in the tall, tall buildings, that Spuddy did not need his shining eyes to guide them. There were no chimneys. All you could see (if you were magic too) was a cloud on which a reindeer with drooping antlers sat, with a potato in a black sooty jacket, a muffler tied round his neck, and a dog with a sack in his mouth. They crept through window after window, and door after door, leaving toys and oranges and sweets and scarves in socks and stockings and pillowcases that were hung at the bottom of beds. They visited all manner of big and small, square and round rooms with sleeping children in them.

They kept going all day and all night, and even though they were up and down, and in and out of houses, Dog carrying the heavy sack of toys all the while, Spuddy and Dog never seemed to feel tired. 'Must be magic too,' murmured Dog between his teeth, taking care he did not drop the sack.

'It is,' said the reindeer with the drooping antlers. 'Father Trickmas is magic, you see, and he passes it on to the cloud, who gives it to you and to me when we sit upon him. It is very strange magic and will last all the time we are helping Father Trickmas.'

'How exciting,' said Spuddy. 'I like magic.'

'So do I,' said Dog, almost forgetting the sack in his mouth.

'Come on. We'd better go. We still have a lot to do.'

4

BRANCHES

They finished their deliveries after two days and two nights. The reindeer with the drooping antlers had worked hard refilling the sack for them and guiding the cloud round the world.

They were gliding above some tall trees and peering over the side, when the reindeer with the drooping antlers suddenly gave a groan and lay down. 'What ever is the matter?' said Spuddy to the reindeer.

'My head. My head. I can't stand it any longer, it feels as though my antlers are dropping off.' No sooner had he spoken than there was a bang and a crash and the reindeer's antlers fell off the cloud, and as they hurtled towards the ground they stuck in the branches of the tall trees.

'My antlers! My antlers!' cried the reindeer. 'They've come off. What am I going to do? I

'My antlers, my antlers,' cried the reindeer. 'They've come off.'

can't go back to the others without antlers,' and he began to cry. He sobbed and he sobbed, huge tears fell through the cloud and landed on the trees below, making them drip like pouring rain.

Spuddy and Dog looked in horror at the state of the reindeer.

'It's a good thing Speedy is not here,' said Dog. 'He would only laugh and say "He's lost his branches".'

'Branches,' shouted Spuddy, jumping up and down on the cloud excitedly. 'Branches, Dog, branches. You are clever,' he laughed.

'Am I?' said Dog in surprise. 'I only said branches.'

'Yes, but that's just it, we are going to have to get some branches for the reindeer.'

'What do I want branches for?' shouted the reindeer, forgetting to cry for a moment.

'For your head, of course,' said Spuddy.

'Oh I see,' said Dog, beginning to understand what Spuddy was thinking.

'Come on, Dog, we must guide the cloud down towards the trees. You lean over and grab some branches with your teeth.'

'I can't carry a sack of toys and grab branches,' said Dog.

'Leave the sack on the cloud. We've finished our work. It's empty, we've no more toys to deliver.'

They coaxed the cloud down and started looking amongst the tall trees for some suitable branches. The reindeer was still wailing, 'My head, my head.'

'Just wait,' said Spuddy, 'we will soon have you looking smarter than all the other reindeer. Stop crying and keep still, otherwise you will topple off the cloud.'

The reindeer was rather surprised at Spuddy's stern voice, and did as he was told.

Dog leant over the cloud, and grabbed the branch.

'There's one,' cried Spuddy. 'Grab it, Dog.' As they drifted past a tall fir tree, they noticed a huge branch with sticking out twigs. Dog leant over the cloud and grabbed the branch. He pulled and pulled. Spuddy wrapped his arms round Dog's middle and held on to him in case he fell off the cloud.

There was a crack as the branch gave way to Dog's teeth, and Dog and Spuddy fell back on to the cloud, Dog with the branch still in his mouth.

'That will do one side,' said Spuddy. 'Leave it on the cloud and let's look for another one.'

The cloud sailed backwards and forwards and Dog and Spuddy peered anxiously over, whilst the reindeer gave little moans as he lay. 'My head. My head,' he cried quietly to himself. 'Oh, how it aches.'

Dog saw another branch and snapped at it. This time Spuddy was not quick enough to grab Dog round his middle, and Dog fell off the cloud, holding on to the branch with his teeth and dangling from a tall tree.

'Hold on,' shouted Spuddy. 'I will guide the cloud down to you. Careful, cloud,' he said as the cloud drifted near to Dog. 'Don't you get stuck in the trees or none of us will find our way back to the Man in the Moon.'

As he spoke the light in the sky seemed to get brighter and brighter, as if the Man in the Moon had heard and was giving them more light to guide the cloud.

'Come on, reindeer,' said Spuddy. 'You have got to help get Dog back on the cloud.'

The reindeer jumped up, forgetting all about his pain, and with a toss of his head that had no antlers, he threw Dog up into the air, and Dog landed back on the cloud with the branch still in his mouth.

'Thank you, reindeer,' said Spuddy, and Dog picked himself up, looking a little shaken.

'Phew, thanks, reindeer with the drooping antlers. Oh sorry, you haven't got any now!' he said, and they laughed. Even the reindeer managed a smile.

'Now come on and we will fix you up in no time,' said Spuddy as he undid his muffler from round his neck. 'Keep still, reindeer.' He lifted one branch on to the reindeer's head, and pulled his muffler, winding the end of it under the reindeer's chin, and tying a bow. He did the same with the

My, you look smart reindeer.

second branch.

Dog got up and shook himself, making the cloud all black with his sooty fur. 'My, you look smart reindeer,' he said. 'You're not the reindeer with the drooping antlers any more.'

The reindeer moved his head up and down, and gazed at the muffler tied under his chin. 'It's red, Spuddy, to match your coat. Well, it would be if you hadn't got it all sooty from the chimneys.'

'We'll soon put that right,' said a deep voice from above, and with that it started to rain and rain.

When Dog looked at Spuddy after a few minutes he cried, 'Your jacket, Spuddy, it's all washed and red again, and your handkerchief in your top pocket is spotted once more.' He laughed, shaking the moisture out of his coat, which landed as black raindrops on the cloud. 'I don't feel cold, do you, Spuddy?'

'No, it's magic,' said Spuddy, sticking out his tummy for no particular reason.

'I have new antlers and a red muffler to match Spuddy's jacket,' cried the reindeer. 'Oh wait till the others see me.'

'Now come on, cloud, let's go back to the Man in the Moon,' said Spuddy, and with a *swoosh* the cloud started to climb higher and higher into the sky.

5

MAGIC

As they drew nearer, they saw the Man in the Moon looking down at them, and just as they were gliding closer and closer to their smiling friend, they heard a swooshing sound.

'Look behind,' said Dog. 'There's Speedy the horse.' As they turned towards the noise they saw 27 reindeer pulling a sleigh through the sky towards the moon, driven by Father Trickmas.

'Hello,' cried Speedy the horse, 'we've been all round the world.'

'So have we,' shouted Spuddy.

'Who is that stranger on your cloud with your red muffler tied under his chin?' cried Speedy, peering at the reindeer with the new antlers.

'It's me,' shouted the reindeer.

'Where are your drooping branches?'

shouted Speedy.

'Antlers,' murmured Dog to himself.

'Fell off my head,' called the reindeer. 'Spuddy has found me some new ones, and I haven't got a headache any more. Speedy, I want to pull the sleigh now, so out of the way.'

'Well thanks,' said Speedy crossly. 'Just because you have new branches on your head doesn't mean to say you have to be rude.'

'Antlers,' said Dog under his breath again, 'and you can be rude too when you want.' He knew that Speedy the horse would always call them branches, and would never mend his ways. But he *had* pulled the sleigh for Father Trickmas, thought Dog, and he's a good friend of mine, so he kept his thoughts to himself.

They all landed on the moon and slid off their cloud. They felt very tired all of a sudden, and whilst Father Trickmas collected the empty sacks and folded them on to his sleigh for next year, 27 reindeer lay down and fell asleep. Lying beside them was a horse, a dog, a potato in a red jacket with a spotted handkerchief sticking out of his top pocket, and one more reindeer, who had huge antlers on his head, securely fixed with a red muffler which was tied under his chin in a bow. The only sound that could be heard was the snoring coming from Spuddy.

'It's very quiet,' said the Man in the Moon.

'Let them sleep,' Father Trickmas replied. 'They have worked so hard, and all the toys have been delivered to the children round the world.' He carefully lifted the sleeping Spuddy and Dog and Speedy the horse on to their cloud and whispered to it. The cloud sailed swiftly and silently away.

The Man in the Moon smiled and Father Trickmas waved goodbye to his friends, even though they were asleep. The reindeer with his new antlers raised his head but he was too tired to say goodbye, and just closed his eyes and lay down on his red muffler.

When Dog woke up he was lying in his kennel, and as he looked outside he saw Speedy the horse cropping the grass nearby.

'Hello, Speedy. I must have been dreaming,' he said sleepily. 'I thought I was on the moon with a large jolly man in a red coat trimmed with fur,' he went on, yawning.

'You were,' said Speedy the horse, 'and

The Man in the Moon smiled and Father Trickmas
waved goodbye to his friends.

with a reindeer with drooping branches.'

'Antlers,' muttered Dog, closing his eyes once more. 'Where's Spuddy?'

'Back under the ground,' said Speedy as he went on eating the grass. 'You'll see him soon. Go back to sleep, Dog.'

Dog got up and shook himself, and as he did so, some black dust flew out of his coat. 'That's funny,' he thought as he lay down and closed his eyes. 'Hmm, magic,' he murmured, and fell asleep.

'Magic,' whispered Speedy the horse. He would never forget flying through the air pulling Father Trickmas's sleigh with 27 reindeer. He loved speed. 'That's why I'm called Speedy the horse,' he said to himself.

Meanwhile in the field down the road there was a slight stirring in the ground, and a snore was heard drifting through the air.

Spuddy is asleep, Speedy smiled to himself, and he too lay down and fell asleep. Above them a cloud sailed by, and a moon shone bright in the sky over their heads. A face looked down at them from the moon. A round, smiling face with white whiskers sticking out all over.

BOOK 2
SPUDDY GOES TO
SCOTLAND

1

ABOVE GROUND

Dog lay by his kennel and Speedy the horse cropped the grass nearby. Dog opened one eye and lifted one ear. He sniffed the air and listened. 'I can hear the tractor, Speedy – come on!' He trotted down the road with Speedy following behind until they reached the field.

A tractor was moving up and down in straight lines and potatoes were tumbling on top of the ground as it went.

'Hooray,' cried Dog, 'it's time to find Spuddy and Rosie and James and Jack and King Edward and his chauffeur and the others.'

Speedy watched as Dog collected up his friends in his mouth, dropping them in a large pile in the corner of the field. The pile yawned and stretched and warmed itself in the sunshine, after being so long under the ground, and soon Spuddy and his friends were ready to follow Dog back to his kennel on the edge of Matchings Town.

Percy was particularly pleased to see Dog, and put his hand on Dog's neck as he walked. Spuddy talked to Rosie, James talked to Jack, the King spoke to his chauffeur and all the little potatoes followed behind chattering excitedly.

'I always like it when we come above ground once more,' said King Edward.

'So do I,' said Spuddy. 'I get excited thinking of the new adventures we are going to have.'

'I like adventures too' said Speedy the horse as he trotted beside Dog. 'Jump on my back all of you and hang on to my mane and get used to riding me, then we can travel far and wide and you won't feel tired.'

All the potatoes gave a leap and landed on Speedy's back and hung on to his long mane, except for Percy. 'Can I ride on your back, Dog?' he said.

'Climb on,' said Dog, 'and cling on to my thick fur.'

Spuddy nearly lost his balance several times, so he stuck out his tummy and

'Can I ride on your back, Dog?'

swayed to the rhythm of Speedy the horse,
and Speedy and Dog trotted along side by
side until they arrived at the edge of Matchings Town. Percy climbed off Dog's back.
Dog went into his kennel and came out with
all their clothes in his mouth.

Meanwhile Speedy the horse bent his

knees and lowered himself. Some of the potatoes slipped over his head, and some clung to his tail and slid off that way. Spuddy tried to look dignified, but landed on the untidy pile of potatoes, and everyone laughed as they stood up and dusted themselves down. Spuddy just stuck out his tummy and smiled.

Dog gave each potato his own clothes, and soon Spuddy was pulling on his red jacket and fluffing out his spotted handkerchief in his top pocket. King Edward placed the crown upon his head and draped his ermine cloak about his shoulders, and the chauffeur flicked on his cap and disappeared.

James stepped into his blue trousers with the flared bottoms, and did them up with his smart belt. Jack put his yellow shirt over his head, and adjusted his gold cuff-links to his wrists, and they sparkled in the sun. Rosie put on her daisy dress and asked Spuddy to do up the zip at the back. Then she helped Percy and the little potatoes on with their clothes.

'Can we go to the seaside again?' cried Percy.

'No we can't,' said the King. 'You lie down with the others and have a rest, whilst we grown-ups have a talk.'

Dog fetched a rug and the potatoes sat down in a circle around King Edward.

2

SETTING OFF

Just as they had settled themselves down for a serious talk, there was an engine noise, and round the corner came the chauffeur, driving King Edward's car. He jumped out and joined them on the rug.

'Spuddy,' said the King in his serious voice, 'where shall we go this time?'

Spuddy cleared his throat and stuck out his tummy, feeling very proud that King Edward should be asking his advice.

'We have your car, King Edward,' he said, 'and we have the balloon that took us over the sea to visit the whales.'

'You have me,' said Speedy the horse.

'And you have me,' said Dog.

'We must decide which mode of transport we are going to use,' Spuddy went on, ignoring the interruptions.

'Mode of what?' said Rosie, looking rather

puzzled.

'Transport,' replied Spuddy sharply.

'Me,' came a snort. 'I'm your mode of transport. You have already tried me out, and Dog can take Percy and any of the other little potatoes. That's his mode of transport, and it will make more room on my back for the rest of you.'

'Well, that seems to be settled then,' said King Edward. 'Chauffeur, you can park my car beside Dog's kennel and look after it whilst we are away.' The chauffeur flicked his cap looking a little disappointed, but he liked the idea of staying with the car. He would clean and polish it and make it shine like Jack's gold cuff-links whilst they were away.

Dog carried the balloon back into his kennel, feeling extremely relieved. He had not told his friend Speedy that he was very frightened of balloons, especially when they were gliding through the sky making a *swishy* noise. He trembled at the thought and his teeth chattered. He much preferred the idea of Percy and the little potatoes riding on his back. 'My mode of transport,' he smiled to himself.

He would clean and polish it.

'Where shall we go?' said Rosie.

'Leave that to me,' replied Speedy the horse, dancing up and down. 'I shall throw my head in the air and my nose will pick up the scent, and that is the way we shall go.'

'Good,' said King Edward. 'I suggest every-one gets some rest before we start out on our new adventure.'

All the potatoes lay down on the rug and soon there was not much to be heard, except the twittering of the birds, the humming of the bees and snoring from Spuddy.

3

BAGPIPES

They woke to a scraping sound, and looked round to find that Speedy the horse was pawing the ground with great impatience.

'Come on, everyone, I'm fed up with waiting,' and he started to dance up and down with excitement. 'I am your mode of transport.'

'Keep still,' said the King. 'Lower your head and bend your knees whilst we all climb on to your back.'

The King scrambled up first, hanging on to his crown with one hand and Speedy's mane with the other, nearly tripping over his ermine robe as he went. Spuddy helped Rosie and then climbed up himself, whilst James and Jack followed, nearly tumbling off Speedy's back as they scrambled aboard. Percy asked Dog to lie down whilst he got the little potatoes to clamber up, and when

49

they were all safely on board he told them to cling to Dog's thick fur.

'We're off,' they cried, waving and shouting. 'Goodbye, chauffeur. See you soon.'

The chauffeur flicked on his cap and waved to Spuddy and King Edward and all the friends.

Speedy the horse galloped away at such a pace that Spuddy and Rosie, King Edward, James and Jack nearly fell off, and Dog found it quite difficult to keep up. 'Slow down, Speedy,' he panted. 'We are not in a hurry, you know.'

'I am,' said Speedy. 'I'm always in a hurry. I'm your mode of transport,' and swishing his tail he disappeared, with all the potatoes holding on very tight.

Suddenly they heard the most extraordinary noise. Speedy the horse stopped abruptly. Dog nearly bumped into him, and Spuddy lost his balance and fell to the ground with a thud.

'Are you alright?' said Rosie, anxiously peering over the side.

'I think so,' said Spuddy as he got up.

'What have we here?' said a voice, and everyone looked round. There stood a man in a brightly coloured kilt with long check socks and a huge beret on his head, and all round him pipes stuck out. He was holding a bag which he was squeezing. Spuddy thought there was something rather familiar about him. He felt that he had seen him before, but he stuck out his tummy and said nothing.

'How do ye do?' said the man, giving a little bow. 'I am Laird MacTrick and this is my friend Maurice Piper.'

A large, smiling potato held out his hand to Spuddy. 'Welcome to Scotland,' he said. He too had a coloured kilt with bright check socks, he too had pipes all about him and he too was squeezing a bag. 'Do you like my bagpipes?'

'Not much,' snorted Speedy the horse as a rather strange noise came forth.

'Don't be rude,' whispered Dog, sitting down for a rest, forgetting that Percy and the little potatoes were still on his back clinging to his fur. They slid off, and Speedy the horse lowered his head and bent his knees and the others clambered down.

'May I introduce you to my friends?' said Spuddy as he pushed Rosie forward and

'I am Laird MacTrick and this is my friend Maurice Piper.'

she gave a little curtsey. 'This is Rosie,' he went on, and the others all gathered round and shook hands, and bowed their greeting.

'Do you live here?' said King Edward.

'Aye,' said Laird MacTrick, 'and I have stables and kennels,' he went on, eyeing Speedy the horse and Dog.

'Could we have a rest?' sighed Dog.

'Of course you can, and some food.'

'Hurry up then,' said Speedy, 'I'm starving.'

'Thank you,' said Dog, a little embarrassed.

'Follow me,' said Laird MacTrick, and off they went.

He led Speedy the horse to a large stable bedded with straw, and a manger full of bran and carrots. He showed Dog to a kennel with a bowl of delicious meat and biscuits, and then walked back to his house.

Well, it was not exactly a house, it was more like a castle with four turrets surrounded by a moat full of water. All that Speedy the horse and Dog could hear was the sound of bagpipes playing, as Laird MacTrick disappeared into his castle.

'What an awful noise,' snorted Speedy the

It was more like a castle.

horse, puffing bran all over Dog as he stuck his head over the stable door.

Dog smiled to himself. He did rather agree but was much too polite to say so, so he licked his bowl clean and drank some water.

4

TATTIE BOGLE

'Will you come to my bothy?' said Maurice Piper to Spuddy and his friends.

'What is a bothy?' asked Rosie.

'It's my wee hoose,' and he led his new friends to a shed in the garden. 'Come in,' he said, smiling. 'What are your names?'

This is Rosie and this is King Edward,' said Spuddy.

Maurice Piper bowed. 'I've always wanted to meet a King,' he said. 'We in Scotland know all about the way you won first prize and became the King. Wait till I tell my friends you are visiting me. They will never believe me.'

'This is James and Jack,' Spuddy went on, 'and this is Percy and the little potatoes.'

'My, what fun it will be whilst you're here,' smiled Maurice Piper. 'A ceilidh, that is what we'll do, we'll have a ceilidh.'

'A ceilidh? What is a ceilidh?' said Spuddy.

'A party, man, a party. We will dance and sing and play the bagpipes. We'll ask the Laird if we can borrow his castle. I'm sure he will agree. Now sit down and rest your feet, for I must warn you about one thing. The Laird is a fine man, but there is only one other person he talks to in his castle, and that is Tattie Bogle.'

'Who is Tattie Bogle?' cried Rosie.

'Why, the scarecrow that lives in the potato field, but spends the wee night hours with Laird MacTrick. Have you no heard of Tattie Bogle?'

'A scarecrow, eh,' said King Edward. 'I would like to meet him.'

'Well you shall. Come on, we'll go over to the castle now and make some arrangements for the ceilidh, and ask the Laird if you can meet Tattie Bogle.'

Laird MacTrick was in the kitchen as the potatoes entered. He appeared to be muttering to himself, but on the other hand he kept looking up as if he was speaking to someone in particular.

'Don't worry,' whispered Maurice Piper,

'he's talking to Tattie Bogle.'

'Well, I can't see anyone,' said Spuddy. 'Where is the Tattie Bogle?'

'Over there, but you won't be able to see him until Laird MacTrick gives you the magic potion.'

'Magic what!' cried Percy.

'Potion. Draught. Och, drink, child, drink.'

Laird MacTrick turned to them. 'Would you like to see my friend?' he smiled.

'Now drink this slowly'

'Oh yes,' cried the potatoes.

'We would indeed,' said King Edward, giving a little bow.

'Well, I doubt if Tattie Bogle has met a King before, so I'll mix you a potion, though I don't do it for anyone mind – only my particular friends.'

He fetched a jug, an onion and some queer-looking powder, and poured hot water all over it. 'Now drink this slowly, each one of you. One sip, mind.'

Spuddy took the cup first and swallowed. His eyes started to smart and tears began to roll down his cheeks. All the others followed, passing the cup round from one to the other until they had all had a sip. Soon the whole of Laird MacTrick's kitchen floor was awash with potato tears. No one spoke or made a sound.

'It's just the onion making you water,' said Laird MacTrick. 'It will pass.'

Suddenly a voice a bit like a croak said, 'Hello friends. I'm Tattie Bogle the scarecrow and I live in a field with potatoes.'

'Hello,' said Spuddy, staring through his tears.

Rosie gave a little curtsey, and all the

'Hello friends, I am Tattie Bogle the scarecrow.'

others said, 'Hello' in a soft voice, staring at this strange creature.

'I am a scarecrow and I stand in the fields and talk to the potatoes when I have nothing to do,' he went on. 'It passes the time. Birds perch on my outstretched arms and we have a bit of a ceilidh.'

'Ah yes, a ceilidh,' said Maurice Piper. 'That reminds me. I have come to talk to you about that, Laird MacTrick. I have decided, with your permission of course, that we should have a ceilidh for our new friends.'

'What a good idea,' said Tattie Bogle, clapping his hands together as bits of straw fell to the ground and his arms flopped about in excitement. Percy and the little potatoes giggled, and Spuddy stuck out his tummy and gave them a stern stare.

'Let's have it in the grounds then every-one can join in and it won't get your castle in a mess,' exclaimed Maurice Piper.

'Fine. Fine,' replied the Laird.

'Go and fetch Speedy the horse and Dog and they can give a hand – I mean give a paw and a hoof – to prepare the grounds. But first they must drink the potion so they too can see Tattie Bogle.'

They all trooped to the stables. Speedy the horse and Dog were fast asleep. 'Wake up. Wake up,' cried Spuddy, 'and drink this.'

'Why?' said Speedy, yawning, 'I've had a

'UGH. How disgusting,' said Speedy.

drink already out of my bucket.' 'Drink,' said King Edward sternly, and Speedy (who was rather nervous of the King) took a huge gulp out of the bucket that was placed on the ground.

'Ugh. How disgusting,' said Speedy the horse, nearly dribbling all the liquid on to the ground, looking very forlorn as his eyes began to water.

'Drink, Dog,' said Percy kindly. 'It won't last long.'

Dog obediently took a few laps with his long tongue. His eyes too began to fill with tears.

'Hello,' said a croaky voice.

Speedy gave a jump in surprise and Dog looked up in amazement. 'Where did you come from?' he said.

'I was here all the time but you can only see me if you drink the potion. My name is Tattie Bogle and I'm a scarecrow from the potato field. I like dogs as long as they treat me with respect,' he said, eyeing Dog nervously, 'and I quite like horses so long as they don't try and eat my arms or my tummy.'

Speedy gave a snort. 'I'm not in the habit of eating stale straw.'

'Be quiet,' said Dog.

5

THE CEILIDH

'Now then,' said Laird MacTrick, coming out of his castle. 'We have a lot to do. Speedy, you come with me and help drag the tree trunks for the men to throw. Dog, you and Tattie Bogle go and spread the word that there is a ceilidh to the folks round and about. King Edward, we need you for the prize-giving. Spuddy and Rosie, as you are used to welcoming people, being Mayor and Lady Mayoress of Matchings Town, perhaps you would stand at the entrance to my castle and shake hands with my guests.'

Spuddy struck out his tummy, feeling very important. He did wonder to himself how Laird MacTrick knew about his being Lord Mayor, but he said nothing. He wished he had his chain of office about his neck. Rosie smiled, wishing she had on her chic French green suit and hat with the feather, but her daisy dress would have to do. She fluffed it out and pulled down Spuddy's red jacket and arranged his spotted handkerchief in his top pocket.

James and Jack were given the task of setting up the stage for the bagpipe band, and Percy and the little potatoes ran hither and thither, banging pegs into the ground and helping Laird MacTrick haul up a great big tent for the ceilidh.

People started to arrive. Spuddy and Rosie welcomed them at the entrance and shook hands with all manner of folk. The men were dressed in tartan kilts with berets on their heads, and the ladies in a variety of pretty, long flowered dresses. Rosie was pleased after all that she had on her daisy dress to blend in with the other guests.

Dog and Tattie Bogle were wandering back, when suddenly Dog stood very still. He looked at the huge tent blowing in the wind and began to shake. It looked and sounded like something else.

'Come on with you,' said Tattie Bogle kindly, putting his straw arm on Dog's head. 'It's no a balloon, just a big noisy tent to keep us dry. Especially me,' he added with a smile. 'If you were made of sacks and straw you'd want to keep dry.'

Dog leaned a little towards Tattie Bogle and said nothing.

Meanwhile, the tent and the grounds around it were filling up with people. The bagpipe band started to play, with Laird MacTrick standing in the middle blowing out his cheeks, and Maurice Piper striding up and down, his kilt swinging and his bagpipes swaying as he blew and blew.

Speedy covered his ears with his hooves. 'What a terrible noise,' he said. 'Oh, I don't know, I'm good at blowing out my cheeks. I wish I could have a go,' said Spuddy.

'You can. You can,' cried Tattie Bogle, and led Spuddy up on to the stage. Tattie Bogle handed him a spare set of bagpipes, and once he had shown Spuddy how to put the pipes over his shoulder and given him a bag to squeeze, Spuddy puffed out his cheeks and blew with all his might.

Nothing happened, and everyone laughed. Then a little groany noise came from Spuddy's bag and soon he was playing pipes with the rest.

Some of the people began to form

Spuddy puffed out his cheeks, and blew with all his might.

squares around crossed swords that lay on the grass, and pointing their toes, and kicking up their legs, they started to dance. Rosie couldn't resist it. Lifting up her daisy dress, she joined the dancers.

Soon every square had potatoes in amongst them. Tattie Bogle and Dog watched, and even Speedy the horse could not help prancing up and down in time to the music. 'It's no so bad eh, Speedy,' said Tattie Bogle, smiling, and Speedy the horse gave a snort and pretended not to hear.

Dog sighed to himself. 'I'll never teach that horse any manners,' he thought, and leant a little closer to Tattie Bogle, not too happy to be inside the tent, which was beginning to sway a little as the wind started to howl.

6

THE STORM

After the dancing had finished, the big men in the crowd went outside, and began to toss the huge tree trunks that Speedy the horse had collected all about the grounds.

'That's a bit dangerous,' Dog remarked as he and Tattie Bogle stood and watched at the edge of the tent. 'Och no. They're tossing the caber. Whoever throws it the furthest wins the prize.'

'How odd,' thought Dog, but was much too polite to say so.

The wind began to blow very hard. Wisps of straw started escaping from Tattie Bogle's sacky tummy, and all the people looked up a little nervously.

Laird MacTrick glanced around him and motioned the other bagpipers to stop playing. The stage was beginning to rock unsteadily. For a moment there was a hush

Whoever throws it the furthest wins the prize.

around the tent, and then with a sudden cracking and a tearing noise, the wind lifted the tent from the ground and it started gliding away in the howling gale.

The wind lifted the tent from the ground.

Dog could not stop trembling, and as the rain began to pour down upon the people, Laird MacTrick shouted at the top of his voice, 'Come to my castle. Come to my castle. Hurry. Hurry.'

They all ran, people and potatoes alike, tumbling over each other as they scrambled through the opening of the great castle doors, pushing and shoving to get out of the wind and the rain. All except Tattie Bogle and Dog. Tattie Bogle became more bedraggled and sad-looking, as the rain drenched his straw arms and legs, and the sacking around his tummy became so wet and heavy that he could not move. Dog was no help. He still shook and trembled. His teeth chattered as the balloon-like tent glided away into the distance. He was unable to move, and no longer could he lean on Tattie Bogle, who was slowly crumpling to the ground.

Speedy the horse trotted up to his two friends. 'Goodness me,' he said. 'What have we here? This won't do at all.'

Tattie Bogle and Dog could not speak, and Speedy the horse could see that his friends were in serious trouble. 'Dog,' he said sternly, 'pick up what is left of that scarecrow in your mouth and follow me.'

'I can't,' said Dog.

'You can and you will,' and Dog was so frightened he did what he was told.

They reached the stables, where Dog laid the limp Tattie Bogle gently on the ground in a bedraggled soaking heap, too weak

Dog lay the limp Tattie Bogle gently on the ground.

even to speak. Dog shook the rain from his coat, and Speedy the horse took complete charge.

'Tear open a little bit of Tattie Bogle's tummy, Dog, and I will fill it with straw from my bed.'

'Together they began to put new life into Tattie Bogle, filling his sacky tummy, his arms and his legs with sweet-smelling straw.

'He needs some bran for his head and a carrot for his nose, and buttons for his eyes,' said Speedy.

Tattie Bogle began to feel the new life in his body, as Dog and Speedy the horse attended to him, filling him with straw and bran and making his face once more like the Tattie Bogle they knew and loved.

'We'll get Rosie to sew up his holes and put in his button eyes,' said Speedy the horse. 'I'll run and fetch her. You stay with Tattie Bogle, Dog.' Dog looked a little nervous but went on pressing straw into Tattie Bogle.

Speedy found Spuddy and Rosie in the castle, comforting the little potatoes, but when he told them what had happened they ran to the stables, Rosie with her sewing basket tucked under her arm. Putting Tattie Bogle over her knee, she repaired all the tears in his sacking.

'Spuddy,' she said, 'can you spare a little piece of potato skin?'

'What for?' said Spuddy in alarm.

'For Tattie Bogle's mouth. He has lost his face. I have two shiny buttons for his eyes in my basket,' said Rosie.

'And here's a carrot I left for his nose,' cried Speedy the horse. 'He just needs a mouth.'

Spuddy took off his jacket and Rosie picked up the scissors from her basket, and as gently as possible she peeled a small

'There. That's done,' said Rosie.

piece of skin from his sticking-out tummy.

'Ouch,' said Spuddy.

'There. That's done,' said Rosie.

Spuddy looked very brave, and Rosie helped him on with his jacket. He couldn't stick out his tummy any more, because it was rather sore.

When Rosie had finished her mending, she stood Tattie Bogle on his feet, and oh how smart he looked. He had even put on weight, and his button eyes shone, and his carrot nose stuck out proudly and he smiled a huge potato-skin smile.

7

PROUD SPEEDY THE HORSE

The storm had blown itself away and so had the tent. All the people gathered round in the castle as Tattie Bogle, sitting on Speedy the horse's back with Dog at his side, entered through the big castle gates, with Spuddy and Rosie following behind.

'Look at me. Look at me,' cried Tattie Bogle. 'Thanks to Speedy the horse, Dog and Spuddy and Rosie, I am back to normal. No, better than normal! I shall never be able to thank them enough. Dog carried me to the stable and Rosie mended me. Speedy the horse gave me straw for my tummy, bran for my head and a carrot for my nose. Rosie sewed up my tears and gave me two button eyes. Spuddy has even given me a piece of his potato skin from his tummy for my mouth. Oh what wonderful friends I have. Now I can stand in the fields

76

and spread out my arms for the birds to perch on, and I can tell all the potatoes the reason why I look so smart.'

Everyone clapped at Tattie Bogle's happiness. He was an old and dear friend to them all.

Laird MacTrick walked up to Speedy the horse. 'You deserve something very special,' he said. Round his neck he placed a tartan ribbon and round his middle a tartan saddle. He pulled on four red socks over his hooves up to his knees, and placed a shining silver bridle over his head. Lastly he gave him a set of bagpipes. Speedy by then was so proud of himself he at once began to blow, and quite a loud noise came forth, and everyone laughed.

Meanwhile Maurice Piper started to take off his tartan kilt and beret. 'These are for you,' he said, turning to Spuddy. 'No other friend of mine would have given up a piece of his skin for a mouth. You shall wear my kilt and my beret to reward your brave self. Every time we look at Tattie Bogle's smiling mouth we shall be reminded of you, Spuddy.'

Although Spuddy could not stick out his

tummy because it was still rather sore, he slipped on the kilt and the beret and he looked the proudest potato in all of Scotland.

'It's time to go home,' said King Edward, turning to his friends. 'My head is beginning to ache.'

'So is mine,' said Spuddy, feeling with his hands the sprouts on the top of his head. Rosie, James and Jack, Percy and the little potatoes all complained that they too were feeling tired and headachy.

They shook hands with Laird MacTrick

He looked the proudest potato in all of Scotland.

and Maurice Piper. 'Thank you. Thank you for giving us such a wonderful ceilidh,' said Spuddy. 'We shall come and visit you again.'

'Aye. Aye, that you will,' smiled Maurice Piper.

They hugged Tattie Bogle, who was clearing his throat and trying to smile a potato smile. 'Goodbye, I'll always have you with me, Spuddy,' he said, his button eyes shining.

Spuddy, Rosie, King Edward, James and Jack jumped on to Speedy's back, and Percy and the little potatoes climbed on to Dog. They waved to their Scottish friends as Speedy the horse galloped out of the castle, followed by Dog.

This time Spuddy could hold on to the tartan ribbon round Speedy's neck, and Rosie clung to the shining new bridle. The others sat comfortably on the tartan saddle. Speedy the horse was so proud of himself that he slowed down and trotted beside Dog. All the towns and villages they passed through on the way home, could see his shining bridle and tartan saddle and his smart red socks, and the town and village folk turned to wave. They knew what had

His shining bridle and tartan saddle and his smart
red socks.

happened, and they cheered Spuddy and his friends.

'What a lovely place Scotland is,' said Spuddy, checking that his beret was firmly on his head and his kilt was buckled round his middle. 'Perhaps we could invite Tattie Bogle to come and stand in our field one day.'

'Whilst you are underground I will go and fetch him,' said Speedy the horse. 'Now hurry, for here is your field and the tractor is waiting for you.'

The potatoes quickly undressed and lay on the ground. Dog gathered up the clothes and Speedy the horse waved goodbye as they trotted back to the kennel on the edge of Matchings Town.

'You were very kind to Tattie Bogle and I'm proud to have such a good friend,' said Dog.

'Thanks,' snorted Speedy the horse. 'It was nothing.' But he tinkled his shining bridle and felt his tartan saddle on his back, and enjoyed looking down at his smart red socks, feeling rather proud of himself.

Later on, all you could hear beside Dog's kennel was an awful groaning sound as

Speedy the horse blew into his bagpipes.

'What a dreadful noise,' said Dog to himself as he lay down and put his paws over his ears.

'What a dreadful noise,' came a voice from underground, and then the earth shook a little, as a group of very happy potatoes lay laughing to themselves.

BOOK 3
SPUDDY GOES TO IRELAND

1

SPEEDY THE HORSE

Dog opened an eye and sniffed the air. Funny, he thought, I can't smell Speedy the horse. He got up, stretched, and gave a yawn. It was rather windy and he heard something flapping on the side of his kennel. It was a piece of paper, and on it was written 'Gone to the horse fair'.

'Fair eh, won't see him for a bit then,' Dog muttered to himself, and trotted away towards the fields, listening to the engine of the tractor as he went.

Potatoes were lying on top of the ground. 'Hello, Dog,' cried Spuddy. 'Quick or we will get taken away. Some of our friends have already gone.'

Dog picked up Spuddy, and then gathered the rest of his friends in a pile. When they were all assembled they ran towards Matchings Town, where Dog's kennel stood.

Dog heard something flapping on the side of his kennel.

'Phew, that was close,' said Spuddy, sitting down with a thump, quite out of breath.

'I was nearly put into a sack,' cried James.

'So was I,' said Jack.

'We all had a narrow escape,' said King Edward. 'You'll have to be a bit quicker another time, Dog.'

'Well, I will if I wake up in time,' replied Dog. 'Speedy the horse usually wakes me with his snorts, but he has gone.'

'Gone!' cried Spuddy. 'Where?'

'Here's the note he left on my kennel,' said Dog, giving it to King Edward.

"Gone to the horse fair." '

'Oh what fun,' shouted Percy the little potato. 'Can we go to the fair too?'

'I don't see why not. The point is, which fair has he gone to?' said Spuddy.

'He'll have gone to Ireland,' King Edward said wisely. 'That is the place for races and horses and fairs, and Speedy has lots of

'He'll have gone to Ireland,' King Edward said wisely.

friends there.'

'Hooray,' shouted Percy and the little potatoes. 'Let's all go to Ireland.'

Rosie was looking very pleased. She had longed to wear her green racing outfit once again, but hadn't had an occasion to do so since her visit to France. She thought it would look fine at the fair. She went into Dog's kennel, and soon came out looking quite the thing in her chic green jacket and skirt, and the hat with the feather in it that Tante Désirée had chosen for her in France.

'You look smart,' said Spuddy, smiling, and he fetched his binoculars and wooden cane with the silver top from the kennel, and tucked it under his arm. The chauffeur flicked on his cap and went to find the car.

'How will we get to Ireland, King Edward?' asked Spuddy.

'Not in a balloon, I hope,' muttered Dog.

'We'll take the car and the ferry,' replied King Edward as he placed the crown upon his head and his ermine cloak about his shoulders.

Spuddy went a bit quiet, remembering his awful trip on the ferry going to France when he had turned rather green, but he stuck out his tummy and said nothing.

James pulled on his blue trousers with the flared bottoms and did up his smart belt. Jack slipped his yellow shirt over his head and made sure his gold cuff-links were securely fastened in his sleeves. 'I wish I had a cane with a silver top like Spuddy,' he said.

'So do I,' replied James.

They all climbed into the car, the King, Spuddy and Rosie sitting in the front with the chauffeur, and the others squeezing into the back with Dog. Percy and the little potatoes were chattering excitedly, not knowing what adventures were before them.

2

CROSSING

The chauffeur drove to the coastal town where a boat was ready to sail, making *'toot toot'* noises. He drove up the ramp and everyone clambered out. Spuddy and Rosie, knowing all about ferries of course, led everyone up the stairs to the top deck. The little potatoes ran from side to side, looking into the sea. Dog sat down with King Edward, whilst Spuddy and Rosie, and James and Jack ordered drinks. The boat gave a *hoot* and sailed out of the harbour towards the open sea.

A large man came and sat beside King Edward. He had on a jaunty green hat and trousers to match, and a smart checked jacket. He had a pair of binoculars round his neck and a cane with a silver top tucked under his arm. 'Top of the morning to you, and where are you off to, Your Majesty?' he

'And where are you off to, Your Majesty?'

said, bowing to King Edward.

'To the horse fair,' replied the King.

'Well, what a coincidence,' said the man, 'so am I. That's a fine outfit you're wearing,' he went on, looking at Rosie, 'and green is the very colour to wear in Ireland. Did you know that?'

'No,' said Rosie, smiling shyly, very

pleased that she had been noticed.

He eyed Spuddy with his binoculars and cane with the silver top tucked under his arm. Spuddy had a funny feeling that he had seen this person before, but he just stuck out his tummy and said, 'My name is Spuddy and this is Rosie, and these are my friends James and Jack. This is Percy and Dog and the little potatoes, and you have already met King Edward.'

'How do you do? My name is Pat-Trick.' And they all shook hands with the man. 'What a party you are,' smiled Pat-Trick. 'I'll be pleased to show you round if you've not been to Ireland before.'

'Thank you,' said King Edward. 'We have actually come to see a particular friend, a horse called Speedy, but we don't quite know where he will be.'

'Not Speedy the horse,' laughed Pat-Trick. 'Why, he's a great friend of mine too, and he'll be taking part at the fair tomorrow. If you've nowhere to stay the night you can all come and lodge with me, and we will go and meet Speedy the horse tomorrow.' The potatoes all thanked him.

When the ferry had landed, after quite a

smooth crossing, the chauffeur went and fetched the car, and they all got in once more. Pat-Trick climbed into the front with King Edward, Spuddy, James and Jack, whilst the others squeezed into the back.

'How do you do? My name is Pat-Trick.'

3

DUBLIN

Pat-Trick guided the chauffeur through the busy streets of Dublin until they were outside a grand house. 'Here we are,' cried Pat-Trick as he jumped out. All the potatoes tumbled out of the car, and Rosie had to smooth her green outfit as it had got rather creased on the journey.

'Now then, supper and a good sleep and you'll be ready for the fair tomorrow,' said Pat-Trick.

'If you will show us our room I will get these little ones to bed,' said Rosie.

'Dog, you had better come with me.' Percy put his hand on Dog's neck and they followed Pat-Trick up the stairs and into a large bedroom, where, what do you think, a four-poster bed stood before them.

The little potatoes jumped up and down in delight. 'We've been in one of these before,' they cried excitedly, and Rosie and Dog dodged round the bed to catch the naughty potatoes and push them under the covers. Dog lay down on the floor beside the four-poster, quite exhausted, and Percy joined him, lying close beside his warm fur.

Meanwhile, Pat-Trick had ordered hot soup for the others, and Spuddy was soon telling their new friend of the many adventures they had had over the years.

'You saw whales!' cried Pat-Trick in surprise and awe.

'Oh yes,' said Spuddy, sticking out his tummy, 'and I was made Lord Mayor of Matchings Town and I went to France with Rosie.'

Pat-Trick listened to all manner of stories which made him laugh and laugh, and Spuddy's tummy stuck out further and further. The stories became longer and more exciting until at last King Edward had to put his finger to his lips to silence Spuddy.

'I hope it will be as exciting in Ireland,' laughed Pat-Trick. 'Now off to bed with you and I'll see you in the morning.'

Spuddy, James and Jack, King Edward and his chauffeur all climbed the stairs and

Pat-Trick peeped in on his way to bed.

joined Rosie and the little potatoes in the four-poster. As Pat-Trick peeped in on his way to bed, the only sound he heard was rather heavy breathing, and a snore coming from Spuddy.

Next morning Dog was the first to wake, and feeling rather hungry, as he had missed the soup from the night before, he crept down into the kitchen. He found some bread and marmalade, which was his very favourite, and just as he was licking the last of the marmalade out of the pot he heard a voice behind him.

'Hello.'

He jumped rather guiltily and looked round. There was a very strange sight. A

He was licking the last of the marmalade out of the pot.

small neat potato with black spots all over him stood in the middle of the room, with his hands on his hips. 'I'm Murphy,' he said. 'You must be Dog. I've heard all about you from Speedy the horse.'

'Oh, do you know Speedy then?'

'Of course I do. He's my friend.'

Just then Spuddy and King Edward came yawning into the kitchen, eyeing the empty marmalade pot. Dog pretended not to notice. He introduced them to Murphy, who bowed respectfully when he saw King Edward with his crown upon his head, and shook Spuddy warmly by the hand.

The others came down, and soon the kitchen was filled with potatoes wanting to meet Murphy, and Murphy was smiling all over his spotty face at seeing so many new friends.

'I like your spots,' cried Percy, laughing.

'Good,' said Murphy. 'I'm glad because I can't get rid of them.'

Dog eyed Percy sternly and Percy went very quiet. He hadn't meant to be rude and he loved Murphy's laughing face.

'When you've finished your breakfast we'll go and join Pat-Trick. He's already at the

'I like your spots,' cried Percy.

fairground talking to the horses and their owners, and he's sure to be with Speedy,' said Murphy.

Rosie saw that all the little potatoes were washed and dressed, and then she slipped into her green racing outfit and joined the others.

4

THE HORSE FAIR

Spuddy felt very grand walking along with Rosie, and he swung his cane with the silver top with one hand and held his binoculars with the other.

'They do look a smart pair,' said James enviously. 'Indeed they do,' replied Murphy. 'Now follow me.'

When they arrived at the fairground, Murphy started to show them all that was going on. Dog and the potatoes stood in the large field and watched the horses. Some were attached to beautiful wagons. They were standing with bags tied round their noses.

'What are you doing?' cried Spuddy.

'Eating my lunch,' replied a large horse with feathery legs.

'Where is your lunch?' Spuddy went on trying to peer into the bag.

They arrived at the fairground.

'In my lunch bag, of course,' and he snorted and sneezed and covered Spuddy with bits of bran and carrot. Rosie laughed and dusted Spuddy down and smoothed out his jacket, and fluffed out his spotted handkerchief in his top pocket.

Other horses were being led round in a ring, whilst men shouted out numbers and another man with a hammer banged it on

'In my lunch bag, of course.'

the table in front of him and said, 'Done.'

'Done what?' said Dog.

'Sold,' said Murphy. 'This is the sale ring. Horses are bought and sold here, it's the biggest horse fair in Ireland.'

'I can't see Speedy,' said King Edward, looking round. 'I wonder where he is.'

Suddenly they saw Pat-Trick hurrying towards them, looking rather anxious. 'Good morning, Spuddy. Good morning, King Edward. I'm afraid I have some terrible news for you, Speedy the horse has gone.'

'Gone!' cried Spuddy. 'Where has he gone?'

'He's been kidnapped.'

'Kidnapped!' shouted King Edward. 'Oh dear me, what a dreadful thing.'

'What does kidnapped mean?' cried Rosie in alarm.

'Taken away,' said Murphy.

'Where to?'

'Who knows. His friends told me he was dragged out of his stable early this morning by some men whose trousers were done up with string,' said Pat-Trick. 'He kicked and neighed and reared and bucked but it made no difference.'

'Kidnapped!' shouted King Edward.

I bet he did, thought Dog, knowing how cross Speedy would be. Dog was very upset. He did not like to think of his friend afraid and alone.

'How do we start looking for him?' asked Spuddy.

'Take me to his stable,' said Dog quietly. 'I will start by using my nose. I have a clever nose, and at times it can be extremely useful,' and with that he followed Pat-Trick and Murphy to a row of stables. Some had horse's heads sticking out of them, and some were empty. Spuddy and the others followed, and Percy and the little potatoes watched, keeping very quiet.

Dog walked into one empty stable and started twitching his nose. 'This was Speedy's stable,' he said. He sniffed the straw and he

'This was Speedy's stable.'

sniffed the floor. He sniffed the walls and standing on his hind legs he sniffed the manger.

'What can you smell?' asked Spuddy.

'Plenty of Speedy the horse, and near the door strange and different smells.' Dog held his head low, his nose almost touched the ground and he started sniffing all along the stables.

'Please find Speedy,' neighed the other horses. 'He was such a jolly friend and we do miss him.'

'I'll try,' replied Dog, and went on following the trail out of the stables, away from the fairground and towards the road and the hills beyond.

Pat-Trick, Murphy and all his new friends followed behind in silence, wondering where Dog would lead them. Spuddy no longer swung his cane with the silver top, and Rosie wished she had on her daisy dress. Her smart green racing outfit was not quite the thing to be wearing when you go looking for a horse on the highways and byways.

The little potatoes started to cry. 'Where are we going?'

'We don't know,' said King Edward kindly,

'just follow Dog and Spuddy and keep as quiet as you can.'

'Don't be frightened, I will look after you,' Spuddy said, sticking out his tummy. He felt a little frightened himself but he was not going to say so. He took Rosie's arm. Pat-Trick and Murphy walked beside King Edward, whilst James and Jack followed behind, with Percy leading the little potatoes.

5

SPOTTED

They had been going for some time when they came to a large bend in the road. 'The smell is getting stronger,' said Dog, 'much stronger.'

Round the corner, moving a little way in front of them was a huge brightly coloured wagon.

'Ooh,' shouted the little potatoes, 'look at that. Isn't it lovely!'

All sorts of people were sitting in the wagon. The men had their brown corduroy trousers done up with pieces of string, whilst the women wore long skirts. The children started to wave to the potatoes and the little potatoes waved back.

'We must be careful,' whispered Murphy. 'Some of these people are my friends and some are not. We'll ask them if they have seen Speedy the horse.'

'No we won't,' said Dog quietly. 'I can smell him. I think he is pulling the wagon but I can't be sure. Wait till we get closer.'

'No, that's not Speedy,' laughed Murphy. 'That horse looks like me. He's got black spots all over him and he's white underneath. What a sight he looks!' and they all began to laugh, except for Dog.

'Piebald,' laughed King Edward.

'Skewbald,' laughed Murphy.

'Be quiet,' said Dog, 'you'll hurt his feelings. It's funny,' Dog went on. 'I can smell Speedy the horse but I can't see him.'

He trotted past the wagon, leaving the others behind, and came up along side the spotted animal plodding dolefully along. He wore large leather blinkers so that he could only see straight in front of him.

'Good morning,' said Dog.

'I don't know what's good about it,' came a glum voice. 'Nothing good for me.'

'Why, what's the matter?' Dog went on.

'I've been kidnapped. I've been painted white and had black spots jabbed all over me, and worst of all, I won't ever see my best friend again,' and the spotted horse began to cry.

He trotted past the wagon leaving the others behind.

'Who is your best friend?' asked Dog.

'Oh, just a dog, but a very nice dog, I will say.'

Good, thought Dog, I'm glad I'm a very nice dog. He knew then, of course, without a doubt that it was Speedy the horse he was talking to.

'I have other friends too,' the spotted horse went on. 'They're potatoes called Spuddy and Rosie, King Edward and his chauffeur, James, Jack, and Percy and lots of little ones.'

Just then a voice behind them said, 'Gee up,' and a very cracky whip landed on Speedy's back. The horse gave a jerk, lifted his head and started to trot.

'You see,' he said, 'this is my life now. I was going to the horse fair to win some prizes, but now I have been taken away, I won't be going there again, and I won't be seeing my friends any more either. I miss my special friend so much,' and he began to cry once more.

As the spotted horse's tears fell to the ground, Dog noticed they were black and white. Looking up, he could see that they had run down Speedy's face, and the spots had turned into black streaks. Oh dear, he thought, if Speedy the horse could see himself now, he would be so upset, and he smiled to himself.

'Now stop that,' said Dog kindly, still not letting Speedy see who he was. 'I might be able to help you get out of this fix, so be patient for the moment and I'll be back.'

'Who are you?' said Speedy, trying to turn his head.

'Oh, just a passer-by,' said Dog as he started walking back to the others.

'It is Speedy the horse,' he said, joining his friends once more, 'but he does not know we are here, and for the moment it is better that he doesn't.' Dog explained that Speedy's blinkers only let him see straight in front of him. 'If he knew we were here he would get too excited,' said Dog, 'and then we would never be able to get him away.'

'Poor Speedy. What are we going to do?' cried Spuddy.

'I have an idea,' said King Edward. 'Pat-Trick, could you go and find my chauffeur at the fair and ask him to drive the car back here?'

'Of course,' said Pat-Trick, and he hurried

away towards the fair.

'Murphy,' the King went on. 'You know these people. Go and chat to them. Keep them occupied until my car arrives.'

'I will,' said Murphy. 'Come and join me, Spuddy.'

Spuddy felt a little nervous but he stuck out his tummy bravely and hurried towards the wagon with Murphy.

6

THE WAGONERS

'Top of the mornin' to you,' called out Murphy, waving to the children. 'Top of the mornin' to you, Murphy, and who is your friend?' they cried.

'Top of the mornin' to you Murphy, and who is your friend?'

114

'Why, this is Spuddy,' he replied, pushing Spuddy forward.

'He's very smart with his binoculars and cane. Where are you going?'

'Well we were going to the horse fair, but we've lost a friend. Have you seen him, by any chance? He's called Speedy the horse, and he's chestnut with a black mane and tail,' said Murphy.

'Sorry, can't help,' shouted one of the men. 'We've only seen this old grey nag with black spots, and as you can see he's a piebald, a bit like you, Murphy,' and they all laughed.

The piebald horse plodded on, pulling the cart slowly with his streaky head drooping even lower, looking very miserable, and then it began to rain.

'Where are you going?' called Spuddy to the children in the wagon.

'Round the highways and byways,' shouted the children. 'Come up and join us, we like potatoes.'

'We love potatoes,' said one of the men, licking his lips.

Spuddy felt rather uncomfortable and moved a little closer to Murphy. Dog, meanwhile, seeing what was going on, quickly walked over to Spuddy and, lifting his paw from the ground, pushed him over in a puddle of water. Spuddy was so surprised, he got up and was just about to open his mouth to say something to Dog, when Dog pushed him over again with his other paw.

'What are you doing?' cried Spuddy, getting up and pulling down his jacket, trying to wipe the mud off him.

'Being very clever,' whispered Murphy.

'I don't see what's clever in knocking me over,' cried Spuddy in a very cross voice.

'You will,' laughed Murphy, 'you will.'

'I'm afraid you wouldn't like my friend Spuddy any more than you like me,' Murphy called to the children. 'Look at him.'

Everyone on the cart laughed and pulled a face. 'Oh my goodness he's just like you, Murphy. He's covered in black spots. No, you're right, you stay where you are.'

Dog moved back towards Rosie, James and Jack and started to gently push them over into more puddles as the rain fell faster and faster. As they got up, rather surprised at Dog, and tried to wipe themselves down, they too looked just like Murphy with black spots all over them. He then did the same to Percy and the little potatoes, who began to cry.

'Don't cry,' said Murphy, 'he is saving your lives.'

Dog, you see, had been walking in Speedy the horse's tears, which had left a black and white trail on the road, and as he gently pushed Spuddy and the others over, he had made them look as though they had black spots all over them just like Murphy.

'They'll never want us in the wagon now,' laughed Murphy. 'They have a hot coal stove in there, and we would have been barbequed by now.'

'What does barbequed mean?' asked Rosie, pulling down her green skirt and wiping herself with Spuddy's spotted handkerchief.

'Burnt,' said Dog, 'and don't do that, Rosie. You need to look as spotted as you can.'

Meanwhile Speedy the piebald horse was still plodding along feeling miserable, not knowing what was going on behind him, for his blinkers meant that the 'straight in front world' was all that he could see. His streaky face dripped on the ground as he went on crying, feeling very sorry for himself.

Just then there was a noise from behind, and turning round, the potatoes watched the chauffeur drive King Edward's car up alongside the wagon, and Pat-Trick jumped out.

'Oh look at that beautiful car,' cried the children, climbing out of the wagon and crowding round.

'Would you like a ride?' said King Edward.

'Oh yes,' and before anyone could say another word, the children were pushing and shoving and squeezing into the car.

'Now, let's have some order here,' said Pat-Trick.

'Chauffeur, you take these children for a few minutes and we will have a word with the grown-ups.'

Pat-Trick climbed into the wagon and began to talk to one of the men whose trousers were done up with string. 'Why don't you all go off for a few days in King Edward's car?' he said. 'The chauffeur will drive you wherever you like. You could have a holiday. We'll look after your wagon for you.'

'What about the old nag?' said the man.

'That's no problem. We'll look after him too.'

It didn't take long to persuade the wagoners, and as soon as the chauffeur returned in King Edward's car, the ladies with the long dresses and the men with their trousers done up with string climbed in beside the children. King Edward spoke to the chauffeur, who seemed rather surprised and perhaps a little put out at being asked to take all these wagoners for a holiday, but he liked a change and soon readily agreed. Off they sped and Pat-Trick and Murphy and Spuddy waved and waved until the car was out of sight.

7

DISAPPEARING SPOTS

Just then there was a crack of thunder and it began to pour with rain. 'Stand where you are for a few minutes,' said Pat-Trick, 'and get really wet.'

'Why?' asked Spuddy, shivering. Then, as he looked at the others he could see why. The rain was washing their black spots. 'Look at us,' he laughed, 'our spots are running away on the ground.'

They all gazed at each other getting cleaner and cleaner.

'Now,' said Pat-Trick, 'I will lift you up into the wagon.' He picked up Spuddy and Rosie first and then the others one by one, until they were under cover. All except Murphy, whose spots didn't disappear in the rain.

'Come on, Dog. Let's go and see Speedy the piebald horse,' he said. 'He won't be piebald any more.'

Sure enough, as they walked past the wagon beside the piebald horse, whose head drooped even lower, his black spots and the white paint ran down his coat, and poured on to the ground as he stood miserably in the rain. Instead of looking like a piebald horse he appeared streaked and terrible. Fortunately he could not see himself or Dog, because of his blinkers and his 'straight in front world', and Dog said not a word.

His black spots and the white paint ran down his coat.

Pat-Trick joined Dog and Murphy. 'Leave him for a while till the storm is over and then we will take off his blinkers, and put him out of his misery,' said Dog. They joined the others, who were in the wagon sitting round the stove drying themselves.

'Isn't this fun!' said Percy.

'Don't get too near, we don't want your skin to bake,' said Rosie nervously.

After a while the rain stopped and the sun came out, and Dog and Pat-Trick, with Murphy tucked under his arm, climbed down from the wagon and walked round to where Speedy the horse stood in a pool of black and white water. His coat shone in the sunshine. Not a sign of white paint and black spots to be seen.

Pat-Trick slid the bridle off Speedy's head, which still drooped to the ground in misery. 'Hello, Speedy,' he cried. 'You do look smart.'

'How do you know I am Speedy? And how can I be smart, painted white with black spots all over me?' Speedy replied miserably.

'Look at yourself!' laughed Pat-Trick.

'I can't. I have blinkers on and can only see a 'straight in front world,' he went on.

Dog walked forward. 'Hello, Speedy,' he said kindly. 'It's me, your special friend.'

Speedy the horse could hardly believe his eyes. He turned this way and that and looked at his shining coat with his black mane and tail.

'Hello, Dog. Hello, Murphy. I thought I would never see you again. Are my other friends here too?'

'They are in the wagon. You must pull a little faster, Speedy, so we can get away from here.'

'Let's go back to the fair,' cried Percy from the wagon.

'Now that's a good idea,' said Murphy, 'then we can mingle with the crowds and Speedy won't be spotted.' Everyone laughed at this remark, even Speedy the horse smiled.

'Spotted indeed,' he said. 'I never want to be spotted again.'

As they set off towards the fair once more, they were just passing a green field, when a white horse with black spots looked at them over a hedge. 'Hello,' he said. 'What a lovely wagon. I have always wanted to pull one of those.'

'Well, you shall,' said Pat-Trick.

'Well, you shall,' said Pat-Trick. 'I will open the gate and you can take the place of Speedy the horse.'

Pat-Trick undid the harness on Speedy's back and put it on the piebald horse. He hitched him to the wagon and once more they were on their way.

'Dog,' he said, 'you and Speedy go on ahead. Murphy will show you the way.'

'Jump on my back, Murphy,' said Dog, and together with Speedy the horse they trotted off towards the fairground.

Spuddy and Rosie were busy in the wagon, smartening themselves up now they were dried off. Percy and the little potatoes were very excited to be off to the fair once more, and Pat-Trick walked beside the piebald horse towards the fairground.

8

GOODBYE IRELAND

They were jostled by the crowds as they made their way between the wagons. There was Speedy the horse tossing his head and dancing and prancing round, his coat shining in the sunlight. The horses thanked Pat-Trick, and Spuddy, and Murphy, and Dog and the potatoes for returning Speedy.

'He will win the competition for the best-turned-out horse,' they neighed at the tops of their voices, and sure enough Speedy the horse galloped past in great style, the winning rosette fluttering on his bridle. Pat-Trick was looking very pleased with himself, and Spuddy and Rosie strolled about looking quite the smartest of all the people at the fair.

Just then King Edward's car drove up and out jumped the wagoners, looking so happy. 'We have had a wonderful holiday,' they cried. 'The chauffeur has driven us all over Ireland at such a speed. Where is our wagon?'

'Here it is,' said Murphy.

'What have you done to the piebald horse? He looks so smart and so happy. He even seems bigger.'

'Yes, he has grown a bit,' smiled Pat-Trick, 'and he has enjoyed himself with us. You don't have to crack a whip at him any more, he will go better without that.'

Suddenly Speedy the horse galloped passed the wagoners, snorting and prancing.

'That's a fine horse,' they said.

'Yes, he's just won a prize,' laughed Pat-Trick. 'Well, goodbye. Thank you for the loan of your wagon. Come along,' he said to the others, and they began to walk away. Dog kept very close to Pat-Trick, and Murphy and Spuddy and Rosie smiled politely to the wagoners, and waved to the piebald horse.

Pat-Trick noticed that the potatoes were beginning to grow shoots on the tops of their heads, and quietly suggested to Murphy that it was time for them all to go back to their homes. He and Murphy waved goodbye to his new friends at the ferry, and after crossing over the sea and driving in King Edward's car back to Matchings Town, they were all quite ready to be planted once more into the ground.

Dog folded their clothes, and as he smoothed out Spuddy's spotted handkerchief from his top pocket, noticed that instead of the spots being white they were black. He smiled to himself as he put them away in his kennel and lay down for a well-earned rest.

Just then he heard hooves clippety clopping down the road. He opened one eye and wagged his tail. 'Hello, Speedy.'

'Hello, special friend,' said Speedy the horse, and he tossed his head and put his nose to the ground, and his rosette waved to Dog.

BOOK 4
SPUDDY GOES TO
WALES

1

SPUDDY'S IDEA

As Spuddy lay under the ground waiting to be dug up once more, he was thinking deep thoughts. 'I would like to climb the highest mountain and look down upon the world,' he said to himself. 'I will speak to King Edward, he is wise. Perhaps we could set up an expedition,' and he tried to stick out his tummy, which was rather difficult underground.

Then he heard the hum of the tractor and felt himself being lifted up, and as he lay for a few moments enjoying the warm sunshine, he was able to stick out his tummy once more.

'Hello, Spuddy,' said James.

'Hello, James. Have you seen Dog?'

'There he is,' and they watched Dog hurrying towards them.

Soon Dog had all his potato friends gathered together, and they followed him out on to the road towards Matchings Town.

When they reached his kennel, Dog fetched their clothes, and Spuddy pulled on his red jacket and tucked his spotted handkerchief into his top pocket. Rosie put on her daisy dress and Spuddy did up her zip at the back. James climbed into his blue trousers with the flared bottoms and fastened his smart belt, and Jack pulled his yellow shirt over his head, and made sure his gold cuff-links were firmly fastened round his wrists. King Edward lifted his crown upon his head and pulled his ermine cloak about his shoulders, and the chauffeur flicked on his cap. Percy and the little potatoes were running round in excitement and Dog was chasing his tail and making them laugh.

Spuddy walked over to King Edward. 'How about climbing a mountain?' he said. 'It's something we've never done before and I'm sure it would be fun.'

'I don't know about fun,' laughed King Edward, 'It would certainly be a challenge. Go and fetch the car, chauffeur, whilst we talk to the others,' and the chauffeur touched his cap and ran towards Matchings

132

Dog was chasing his tail and making them laugh.

Town.

They all discussed the climbing of mountains as they sat warming themselves in the sunshine, but after listening for a while, Rosie suggested that she should stay behind with Percy and the little potatoes, and go on helping them with their reading and writing.

'Oh,' cried Percy in disappointment, but

Dog leant against him gently and whispered to do as he was told. Percy sighed and gave Dog a hug. He knew Dog was always right, and perhaps he had better help Rosie with the little ones. 'I'll stay,' he said, 'just like I did when Spuddy, and King Edward, and James and Jack visited the whales with the chauffeur in a balloon.'

'Wales!' cried King Edward. 'That's an idea. Thank you, Percy. That's where we shall go.'

'But we have been to see the whales already,' said Spuddy.

'No, Wales,' laughed King Edward, 'Wales, the land of mountains and hills and rushing rivers.'

'And rain,' said Dog quietly.

'Not the whales that live in the sea,' King Edward went on. 'You will come with us, won't you, Dog?'

'And so will I,' cried a voice as Speedy the horse came galloping up, stopping just in time before he knocked everyone over.

'Well, that's settled then,' said King Edward. 'We'll get the chauffeur to drive us to Wales, the land of mountains and hills and rushing rivers' ('and rain,' whispered

Dog under his breath) 'to the bottom of the tallest mountain. Speedy, you and Dog could start off now and we will meet you in the car when the chauffeur gets back.'

Speedy the horse tossed his head and pranced away on his four fine hooves, and Dog, not sure whether he agreed that climbing mountains was the best way to pass the time, followed reluctantly behind. He was a kindly fellow and did not like to disappoint anyone. The others sat down to wait for the chauffeur and King Edward's car, and when it came round the corner they scrambled in and waved goodbye to Rosie and Percy and the little potatoes.

2

MOUNT SNOWDON

They drove through the night, and just as the sun was beginning to rise and shine in the sky, they saw Speedy the horse and Dog trotting beside him along the road.

On either side the mountains towered above them, and they came upon one that was huge and magnificent, the top of which was hidden in mist.

'Mount Snowdon,' said the King wisely. 'Mount what?' cried Spuddy.

'Snowdon.'

'Why is it called that?'

'Because it has snow on the top, silly,' snorted Speedy the horse.

'And always looks white,' the King went on.

'Up we go,' said Speedy the horse impatiently.

'Wait, said Dog. 'We must prepare ourselves. You can't just walk up a mountain, you know.'

'No you can't,' said a voice, and out of the mist came a very tall, thin figure, wearing

'My name is Mr Leekatrick and I am a mountain guide.'

huge boots with cords of rope looped round his middle.

'How do you do?' said Spuddy, getting out of the car. 'My name is Spuddy and these are my friends,' and they all shook hands with the tall figure.

'My name is Mr Leekatrick and I am a mountain guide,' said the man. Spuddy had the strange feeling that he had seen this man before, but he stuck out his tummy and said nothing.

'And I'm Taffy Tate,' laughed a jolly figure standing beside Mr Leekatrick, 'and I'm a potato,' and he bowed as he saw King Edward with the crown upon his head.

'Mr Leekatrick likes me with him because I can bounce down the mountains if anyone needs rescuing, and stay with them until Mr Leekatrick can pull them up with his rope. We are a good team.'

'Oh, we won't need rescuing,' cried Speedy the horse, pawing the ground, and he started up the mountain at a gallop. Dog kept quiet. He knew a bit about steep hills, and was glad of his claws to stick into the mountainside.

'Do you all want to go up the mountain?'

'I can bounce down the mountains if anyone needs rescuing.'

asked Mr Leekatrick.

'Oh yes please,' cried the potatoes.

'Good. Now wind the rope firmly round your middles,' he said, 'and keep one behind the other, and if any of you want to stop for a rest, just pull gently on the rope and we will wait. Dog, you take the end of the rope and keep behind in case of an accident.' So Dog put the rope into his mouth, pleased that he was being made part of the team.

They waved goodbye to the chauffeur, who decided to stay with the car at the bottom of the mountain, and then Mr Leekatrick strode out in front, and Taffy Tate whistled, whilst the others kept in time with his merry tune, placing one foot in front of the other, climbing higher and higher.

'That horse is going much too fast,' said Mr Leekatrick. 'He'll get out of breath.'

He'll get out of anything, thought Dog as he walked quietly behind the others with the rope firmly clenched between his teeth.

The mist was beginning to gather round them and Dog could not see his friends in front. He was feeling rather damp and cold, and his soggy wet coat clung to him. Mr Leekatrick was encouraging the others. 'Come on, my friends, you are doing well, nearly there,' and Taffy Tate's merry tune drifted back to Dog. It was an eerie feeling, rolling mist, round shadows and in the distance galloping hooves from above.

Climbing higher and higher.

3

A TERRIBLE CRASH

'It's getting colder,' said Spuddy, pulling his red jacket tightly round his middle. The others were very quiet. Except for the heavy breathing of the climbing potatoes, the only sound that could be heard through the mist was Speedy the horse snorting.

Suddenly Mr Leekatrick stopped and turned and said quietly, 'Here we are.' The mist had cleared and there below them was the world, and on the top of the mountain where they stood, snow lay, looking very white and very beautiful.

Spuddy could hardly believe his eyes. He gazed and gazed at the beauty all around him, and even Dog, who did not really enjoy climbing mountains, was in awe of all he saw.

'Isn't it quiet,' whispered Jack.
'So peaceful,' said James.

'I feel I am on top of the world.'

'I feel I am on top of the world,' said
Spuddy, sticking out his tummy.

'You are,' laughed Taffy Tate, and they all
looked round in silence.

The potatoes found a ledge to sit on, and Dog stretched out in front of them so they could not fall down the side of the mountain by mistake. Potatoes roll, he thought, and could easily bounce all the way down.

King Edward sat by Taffy Tate, and as they were talking quietly to each other they heard a voice shout from above, 'Look at me, look at me!' They all looked up, and there was Speedy the horse prancing through the clouds.

'He's showing off as usual,' said Dog.

'He'll slip if he is not careful,' cried Taffy Tate, and no sooner had he uttered those words, than there was a terrible *crash*.

Down the mountainside, tumbling over and over, came flaying hooves as Speedy the horse bumped past them, hitting his back, his neck and his head on the hard rocks. 'Help,' he cried, 'help me,' and he flashed past Mr Leekatrick, gathering speed. He nearly squashed poor Taffy Tate, who jumped out of the way just in time. Spuddy threw himself to the side, tearing his red jacket on a jagged rock as he did so. King Edward lost his crown in the scramble to get away, and poor James and Jack were hit by

Taffy Tate jumped out of the way – just in time!

a flying hoof, and tossed down the mountainside after Speedy the horse.

145

Dog gripped the rope between his teeth and held on as tightly as he could.

The rope that held them together suddenly became very taut and poor Spuddy's tummy, instead of sticking out, was being squeezed and squeezed. Mr Leekatrick, Taffy Tate, Spuddy and King Edward flashed past Dog as they tumbled and bounced down the mountain. Dog, in the nick of time, dug his claws into the side, and with all his might gripped the end of the rope between his teeth and held on as tightly as he could. Then there was silence. The mist was creeping round again and Dog felt very alone.

4

ALL SAFE

'Anyone there?' came a voice.

'Yes,' said Dog between clenched teeth.

It was Spuddy. His red jacket had got caught on a rock and saved him from tumbling down the mountain with the others. He got up, and when he had unhooked his jacket from the rock and pulled it round himself adjusting the rope, he looked about him.

'Come on, Dog,' he said quietly, 'we must try and find the others,' and putting his hand on Dog's neck, they very slowly and very carefully started to feel their way, following the rope down the mountain.

'What's that?' said Spuddy, seeing something lying hooked over a rock, like his jacket.

'It's King Edward's crown,' cried Dog, and then there was a movement close by.

Dog scrambled over the rocks and Spuddy started coiling up the rope just as he had seen Mr Leekatrick do earlier in the day. Dog gently nuzzled King Edward, who looked up and smiled.

'Hello, Dog. Are you alright?'

'I am,' said Dog. 'How about you?'

'A bit wobbly. Have you seen my crown?'

'A bit wobbly, have you seen my crown?'

'Here it is,' said Spuddy, as Dog fetched it, and once King Edward had placed it back upon his head he felt very much better.

'Where are the others?' he asked.

'We don't know, we are trying to find them,' said Spuddy.

King Edward hitched the rope round his ermine cloak and, very gently, holding on to Dog's neck, one each side, they went on scrambling and slithering and sliding down the mountain. As they went, rocks and boulders crashed before them.

Next they found Mr Leekatrick, who appeared through the mist, a ghostly figure looking a little shaken.

'Now then,' said Mr Leekatrick, 'I think we had better find James and Jack.'

'And what about Taffy Tate?' cried Spuddy.

Just then they saw Taffy Tate sitting on a rock, rubbing his head.

'Thank goodness,' said Spuddy. 'Are you alright? Can you manage to walk?'

Taffy Tate laughed. 'Oh yes, I'm used to tumbles, but not quite as fast as that, I must admit,' and he got up and shook himself to make sure he was all in one piece.

They all climbed down the mountainside in silence. Spuddy was very worried about his friends. Their rope must have broken and he was imagining all sorts of dreadful things that could have happened to them.

As the mist lifted a little, and swirled around, they saw two battered and bruised potatoes lying in a heap. One of James's

They saw two battered and bruised potatoes lying in a heap.

blue trouser legs was badly ripped, and Jack's shirt lay in a bedraggled heap beside him. They did not stir. Mr Leekatrick lifted them and gently laid them on Dog's back. Their potato skins were torn, and hung down in sad dripping strips. All the others stood around and were very quiet.

Mr Leekatrick coiled up his end of the rope and gave Dog the other end to hold fast in his mouth. 'Now steady, Dog,' he said. 'Go down as gently as you can, and we will follow.'

Spuddy picked up James's trousers and Jack's torn shirt and held on to Dog's neck as they followed him down the mountain. All was quiet except for the moans and groans coming from Dog's back.

Spuddy tried not to think about what it would be like without his two dear friends James and Jack, and clung to Dog and stumbled and slipped, hardly noticing where he was going.

'That's a good sign,' said Taffy Tate cheerfully.

'What is?' said Spuddy.

'That they can moan and groan. It means they are alive and we will soon have their

All was quiet, except for the moans and groans coming from Dog's back.

skins back on again, as good as new.'

Spuddy did not know how their skins would mend, and though he tried to stick out his tummy, it hurt too much from being squeezed by the rope, so he continued in silence.

5

A STRANGE DREAM

It took a long time to reach the bottom of the mountain, but eventually they did, and Dog dropped the rope out of his aching jaws. Mr Leekatrick gently lifted James and Jack off Dog's back, and laid them on the ground. Dog sat down, too exhausted to speak, and his paws were bleeding from clinging to the mountainside. He licked them because he knew his tongue would heal his wounds, and then he fell asleep.

'James and Jack must get over the shock first,' said Mr Leekatrick kindly.

Spuddy went over and sat close to his friends, and Taffy Tate began to hum a soft melody. King Edward sat down beside Spuddy.

A strange feeling came over Spuddy. He closed his eyes and lay listening to Taffy Tate's tune. King Edward did the same.

Spuddy thought he saw Mr Leekatrick stand beside him and lift his long arms above his head, moving them back and forth over his two friends. King Edward thought he saw their tattered skins slide back into place as good as new. Spuddy thought he saw James get up and pull on his blue trousers with the flared bottoms, and do up his smart belt. King Edward thought he saw Jack sit up and pull his yellow shirt over his head, and fasten his shining gold cuff-links about his wrists. And all this time they heard a humming tune.

Then they woke and opened their eyes, and the two friends, James and Jack, were sitting up smiling at them. 'Hello, Spuddy. Hello, King Edward. We have had such a funny dream,' they said.

They told them how they had dreamt of falling down the mountainside. How they hurt a great deal. How they had felt themselves lifted up and laid on something soft. How a tall man with a rope wound round his middle had stood over them, waving his arms about, and how they heard a sort of humming noise. Then they woke up to find they were sitting beside Spuddy and King

Edward, as good as new.

'Where are Mr Leekatrick and Taffy Tate?' asked King Edward, looking round.

'Nowhere to be seen,' said Spuddy.

'There's Dog,' said Jack. 'He looks tired. I wonder what he has been up to, and why is that long rope lying beside him? and why are his paws bleeding?'

'I think you had better listen,' said King Edward wisely, 'whilst Spuddy tells you what has been happening.'

The four friends sat close to the sleeping Dog, whilst Spuddy told of their adventures up the mountainside with Mr Leekatrick and Taffy Tate. James and Jack remembered nothng.

'Concussed,' said King Edward wisely. 'Con– what?' said Spuddy, sticking out his tummy, forgetting how much it hurt. 'Cussed,' went on King Edward.

'Oh, concussed,' repeated Spuddy, sticking out his tummy even more, because he did not know what concussed meant.

Just then Dog woke up and gave a huge yawn and stretched out his front paws that were still a little swollen.

'Hello,' he said. 'I have just had the strangest dream. There was this tall man with a rope wound round his middle and a sort of humming tune ...'

'Yes. Yes,' said King Edward. 'I think we had better go and find the chauffeur and the car,' and they all got up and started walking down the road, Dog limping a little as he went.

'I have just had the strangest dream.'

6

HOME

The chauffeur was standing beside the car, waving his cap and jumping up and down. 'I am pleased to see you,' he cried. 'I have been asleep and have had the strangest dream. There was this tall man with a rope wound round his middle and a sort of humming tune ...'

'Yes. Yes,' said King Edward, laughing. 'Get in, everyone, and drive on, chauffeur.'

They all jumped in and just as they came round the corner, there was Speedy the horse lying across the road sound asleep.

'Hello,' he said, opening his eyes sleepily. 'I have just had the strangest dream. There was this tall man with a rope wound round his middle and a humming tune ...'

'Yes. Yes,' they all laughed. 'Get in, Speedy, we are going home.'

'Ow,' said Speedy the horse as he jumped

up. 'I have bruises all over me.'

'And I have sore paws,' said Dog.

The chauffeur drove back to Matchings Town, where they soon joined Rosie and Percy and all the little potatoes. Rosie clapped her hands when they all jumped out of the car.

'Oh thank goodness,' she said. 'I am so pleased to see you all. We have been asleep and had the strangest dream. There was this tall man ...' she began and the others cried out, 'With a rope wound round his middle, and a humming tune ...'

'How do you know?' she cried in surprise.

'We just do,' said Spuddy, sticking out his tummy, which didn't hurt any more. 'Come on, it's time we went back to the field. Take off your clothes and give them to Dog. Goodbye, Dog. Goodbye, Speedy. See you next year.' They all walked towards the field where once more the tractor was moving up and down making rows, and men were planting potatoes into the ground.

'I wonder if there really was a tall man with a rope wound round his middle, and a merry tune,' said Spuddy as he lay down whilst earth was sprinkled over him.

As Dog trotted back to his kennel he wondered why his teeth were loose and his paws rather swollen. Speedy the horse was very quiet. He felt a bit battered and bruised, but the two friends didn't say anything to each other, just kept their thoughts to themselves.

Somewhere far away in the land of mountains and hills and rushing rivers (and rain), stood a tall man with a rope wound round his middle, and beside him was a jolly potato humming a merry tune as they started to climb up the mountainside.

Humming a merry tune, as they started to climb up the mountainside.